HUDSON
To The Rescue

by L.E. KOCOT

Illustrated by Javier Duarte

Wasteland Press

www.wastelandpress.net
Shelbyville, KY USA

Hubert To The Rescue
Written by L.E. Kocot
Illustrated by Javier Duarte

First Edition – December 2019
ISBN: 978-1-68111-339-5

Printed in the U.S.A.

To Seamus
Love
aunt Geri
xoxoxo

Hubert Says This Book Belongs To

♡ Seamus ♡

Enjoy the New Adventures
Of Hubert ☺

Loraine Kocot
♡

It was a cool bright sunny morning as Hubert awakened. With a smile on his face he started his morning off with his special song.

One, Two, I love you
Three, Four, open the door
Five, Six, let's do some tricks
Seven, Eight, clean your plate
Nine, Ten, let's do it again!

This song is what starts Hubert off with a positive day, every day. You can always hear him singing this every morning and sometimes throughout the day too!

Hubert has his usual routine, which is heading to his beautiful field of flowers. He happily skips along the pathway, enjoying his walk to the field.

U pon arrival he was so amazed how beautiful his flowers were. He walked around the entire area looking at the beauty around him. He noticed two pretty butterflies with one resting on a flower and the other flying towards him. "Good morning and how pretty you are" he said.

Hubert spent several hours there before his work was done and that is why he visited this area first. He was so proud of his beautiful garden and it made him very happy. Before leaving the area he smiled and said, "I love you to the stars and back," my beautiful field of flowers!

As he was leaving he began to skip and smile brightly. Oh what a beautiful day this will be, he thought. As he walked along he then heard very loud sounds coming from the bird house. "Chirp, Chirp, Chirp," cried the birds! Hubert immediately began to run and then started to fly as he made his way quickly to the tree house. Hubert's color changed to blue, because he needed to feel strong as he rushed to the rescue.

He arrived just in time to see a little bird falling from his nest. He stretched out his long tail and caught the little bird. He was relieved when he saw the baby bird resting safely on his tail.

The little bird was happy Hubert arrived in time to catch him. Hubert looked at him and said "it is not your time to fly yet little one." He looked up to see the bird family perched on the branch and smiling.

He says, "Everything is fine mommy bird and I have your little one safe and sound." He flutters up to the top and smiles at her. He places the baby bird on the branch with his family. "There you go," he said.

The bird family was now quiet once again and they all smiled at Hubert, because they were happy he was there to save the day. He looked at them, smiled and said "you are all so welcome."

That was a close call he thought. It was then Hubert smelled smoke. From his perch high up in the tree Hubert could see where the smoke was coming from. "Oh dear, what is happening!" he said.

He knew where there is smoke there is fire and immediately headed to Farmer Jack's barn. Flying down from the tree Hubert could see a small fire surrounding the barn.

He quickly flew over the area to spray water to put out the fire.

Hubert felt lucky to be a water breathing dragon. As he approached the barn, he heard three loud squeals, "Oink, Oink, Oink!" Hubert rushes to open the barn door and out comes two cute pink piglets.

"Hello little ones, run as fast as you can!" he said. The yard was starting to fill with smoke and as Hubert began to spray, a beautiful white horse galloped out of the barn.

Hubert was happy to be here to save the little piglets and the beautiful horse too! He immediately sprayed more water inside the barn.

In no time at all, Hubert put out the fire and all was looking good. Even Farmer Jack's crops were okay and Hubert felt so proud to have been here to help. Before leaving, the beautiful white horse came to Hubert and bowed to him.

It was his way of saying thank you for the rescue. Hubert looked happy, smiled at the white horse and said "Thank you, you are very welcome my friend and he hugged him!"

Hubert went to the edge of the path and sat down to wait for farmer Jack.

As he sat under a tree he saw someone quickly approaching the barn, and yes, it was farmer Jack. Hubert watched him as he stood there with his hand on his head looking completely in shock.

As he walked around his farm checking the crops, he wondered how the fire started. Hubert watched as farmer Jack knelt down and heard him say, "Thank you whoever you are for saving my farm."

Hubert began to smile as he continued to look on. Oh how he felt so happy now. He was proud of himself for saving the day for farmer Jack too!

Hubert was so excited and happy with all the good he did and that is when his color gently changed to purple, as he rested calmly under the tree.

Hubert quietly left the area, because he knew now all was well. As he made his way back to the bird family to say good night his color was green again. It was such a busy day and a long day. Time flies so quickly when you are that busy, he thought.

All was quiet with the birds and he felt it was time for his rest. He needed to sleep. As he lay comfortably under a tree he sang his wonderful night time song.

One, Two, I love you
Three, Four, close the door
Five, Six, no more tricks
Seven, Eight, I cleaned my plate
Nine, Ten, I'll see you again

After singing his song he felt so relaxed and started to think about his family and how proud they would be when he told them how he saved the day for many of his friends. He smiled brightly as he looked up to the stars. Soon he would be ready to fall asleep. He laid quietly under the tree smiling as he knew he would slowly drift off to sleep.

THE END

Blue Hubert — Caring Hubert turns Blue to feel Strong when helping friends in need

Purple Hubert – Fun Loving Hubert turns purple when he becomes Happy and Excited.

Green Hubert – Positive Hubert stays natural green when he is relaxed....

Color with
HUBERT

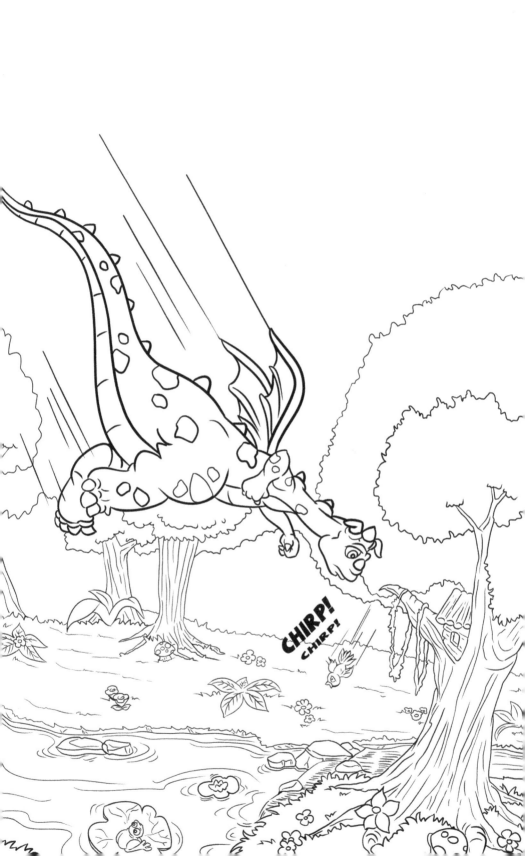

CPSIA information can be obtained
at www.ICGtesting.com
Printed in the USA
LVHW050304201219
640997LV00003B/3/P